The Adventures of Celia Kaye

Written by Kaitlin Puccio

Illustrated by Sarah Larnach

BENT FRAME

New York

It was the first day of school after summer break for Celia Kaye. She was usually very excited to see all her friends, but not today. Today, Celia Kaye did not want to go to school.

"Celia Kaye, you're going to be late for school. What have you been doing up there?" her mother said to her when she went downstairs for breakfast.

"Oh mummy, I *can't* go to school today. I forgot how to speak English!"

Celia Kaye's mom looked at her lovingly. "In that case, should we sign you up for after school English classes?"

Celia Kaye shook her head and put her lunchbox in her backpack. Usually she was very excited to trade snacks at snack time, but not today.

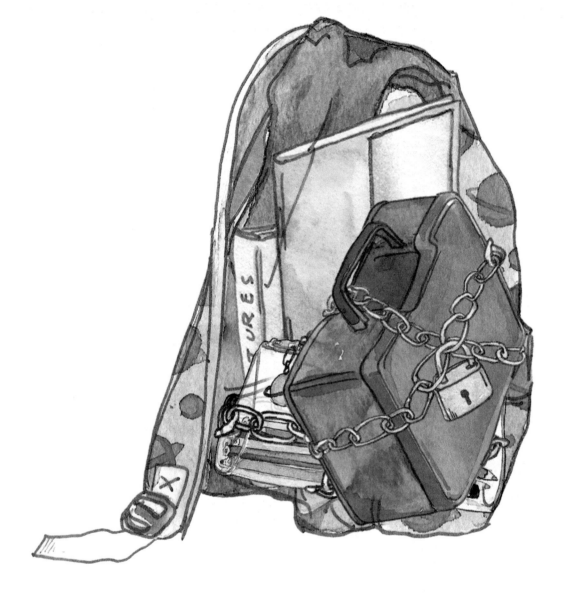

She didn't want to share her lunch, her snack, or even her pencils. She didn't want to talk to anyone at all, because she was afraid they would find out her secret.

It was a new secret for Celia Kaye. It was a secret that she didn't want anyone to know.

At school, Celia Kaye's friends were all sharing first-day-of-school cupcakes. When little Cindy asked Celia Kaye if she wanted a vanilla cupcake, Celia Kaye looked away.

"No thank you Cindy," Celia Kaye began. "I've already had three cupcakes today for breakfast. My mom took me to the bakery before school. We actually went to a bakery in the middle of the ocean. We had to take a boat there. I met a pirate and everything!"

Celia Kaye knew she wasn't telling the truth, but Cindy looked excited. "Wow, you get to have cupcakes for breakfast? My mom would never let me do that! Want to go on the playground with me today?"

Celia Kaye was happy that Cindy believed her. She didn't want to have to tell Cindy her secret. Cindy might have laughed at her instead of invited her to the playground.

After Cindy finished her cupcake, Cindy and Celia Kaye went out to the playground together. "My mom packed me crackers and peanut butter for a snack. Since you didn't eat any cupcakes, do you want some of my crackers?"

"No thank you Cindy," Celia Kaye started. She was so happy to have such a nice friend that she knew she couldn't share her secret. If she did, she was sure she wouldn't have any friends at all.

"One time when I ate peanut butter, my mouth got stuck closed, and I had to go on a journey all the way to France to have the King fix it. I can't eat peanut butter right now. The King is away on vacation and no one else is powerful enough to get peanut butter unstuck."

"Wow," Cindy said. "You met a king? Do you just want some regular crackers instead of crackers and peanut butter?"

"Oh, I don't like regular crackers. The only crackers I like are made on Mars. My mom has to pick them up from the top of the highest mountain in the world when the Martians send them down to me."

Cindy laughed when Celia Kaye finished telling her story.
"Tell another one!" Cindy said. She liked Celia Kaye's stories.

"It's true," said Celia Kaye, but she started to worry that Cindy didn't believe her. "They can't throw the crackers far enough to get them all the way to my house, so my mom has to climb to the top of the mountain every time they make new ones for me."

"That's not true Celia Kaye. There's no such thing as Martian crackers," Cindy said. Cindy didn't like that Celia Kaye was trying to pretend her stories were true. "Martians don't exist Celia Kaye. They can't make crackers for you if they don't exist."

Celia Kaye wanted to tell Cindy the real reason that she wouldn't eat her cupcakes or crackers. But she didn't want Cindy to know her secret.

When Cindy started to walk away from the playground, Celia Kaye got worried. She didn't want her friend to be mad at her. "Cindy!" Celia Kaye called. "Wait!"

Cindy stopped and waited for Celia Kaye. "I don't eat cupcakes or crackers because I can't eat regular foods," Celia Kaye said.

"Why not?" Cindy asked, not sure if she should believe Celia Kaye. After all, Celia Kaye did tell a lot of stories.

Celia Kaye knew she had to tell Cindy her secret. "I have something that makes me not be able to eat certain foods. It's called celiac. It means I can't eat foods that have wheat, rye, or barley in them."

Cindy smiled at Celia Kaye. "It's okay Celia Kaye, I can bring carrots tomorrow instead of crackers so we can share."

Celia Kaye was so relieved that Cindy didn't think her secret was weird. She wanted to tell everyone her secret!

"I'm sorry I told you things that weren't true Cindy," Celia Kaye said looking away.

"It's okay Celia Kaye. I'm still your friend. But why can't you eat wheat?"

Celia Kaye was happy to have a friend like Cindy. "Well," said Celia Kaye. "I can't eat wheat because people who have celiac are from outer space, and have special powers that are taken away if they eat wheat, and…"

The next day Celia Kaye couldn't wait to go to school.